Dear Parent:
Your child's love of reading starts here!

Every child learns to read in a different **way and** at his or her own speed. Some go back and forth between reading levels and read favorite books again and again. Others read through each level in order. You can help your young reader improve and become more confident by encouraging his or her own interests and abilities. From books your child reads with you to the first books he or she reads alone, there are I Can Read Books for every stage of reading:

SHARED READING
Basic language, word repetition, and whimsical illustrations, ideal for sharing with your emergent reader

BEGINNING READING
Short sentences, familiar words, and simple concepts for children eager to read on their own

READING WITH HELP
Engaging stories, longer sentences, and language play for developing readers

READING ALONE
Complex plots, challenging vocabulary, and high-interest topics for the independent reader

I Can Read Books have introduced children to the joy of reading since 1957. Featuring award-winning authors and illustrators and a fabulous cast of beloved characters, I Can Read Books set the standard for beginning readers.

A lifetime of discovery begins with the magical words "I Can Read!"

Visit www.icanread.com for information
on enriching your child's reading experience.

Funding for MOLLY OF DENALI is provided by the Corporation for Public Broadcasting and by public television viewers. In addition, the contents of MOLLY OF DENALI were developed under a grant from the Department of Education. However, those contents do not necessarily represent the policy of the Department of Education, and you should not assume endorsement by the Federal Government. The project is funded by a Ready To Learn grant (PR/AWARD No. U295A150003, CFDA No. 84.295A).

www.icanread.com

ISBN 978-0-06-295040-6

Book design by Brenda Echevarrias-Angelilli and Chrisila Maida

20 21 22   CWM   10 9 8 7 6 5 4 3   ❖   First Edition

I Can Read!

1 BEGINNING READING

MOLLY OF DENALI™

Crane Song

Based on a television episode
written by Princess Daazhraii Johnson

HARPER
An Imprint of HarperCollins*Publishers*

Hey, everyone, it's Molly!

My dad and I are going on a trip
with my friend Nina.

Nina is a journalist.

She takes pictures

and writes about nature.

Dad and I are going to help Nina
with a story about tracking
baby sandhill cranes.
Cranes are one of my favorite birds!

To track cranes,
scientists carefully put metal bands
on the legs of adorable baby cranes.
The bands help keep track
of where the cranes go.

I feel a tap on my shoulder.

It's Nina!

She looks like an astronaut!

"I'm supposed to look

like I'm a crane," Nina explains,

"so I won't scare the birds away."

A scientist named Dr. Antigone
is coming on the trip, too.
My job is to hand her banding tools
when she catches baby cranes.

"Let's get going," says Dad.
"Those baby cranes won't wait
forever!"

Once we're at the lake,

we have to be very quiet.

We don't want to scare the cranes.

But when we get close, I hear

SLAP! SLAP! SLAP!

The noise scares the birds away.

A beaver is slapping his tail

on the water.

We're too close to his home,

so he's trying to scare us away.

What can we do now?

Dad has a suggestion.

He says beavers love

to eat birch tree saplings.

A sapling is a young tree.

We put saplings out for the beaver.

That will keep him busy!

"Let's go band some cranes!" I say.

We approach the cranes again.

But when we get close, I hear:

AAAACHOO!

Dr. Antigone sneezes super loud!

The cranes run away again.

We decide to go to our campsite.

Dr. Antigone needs to rest

and have some tea.

"Why do we need to track cranes?"
I ask Dr. Antigone.

"To learn how cranes migrate,"
says Dr. Antigone, showing me a map.
Cranes fly to Alaska in the summer
to have their babies.
Then they fly south in the winter.

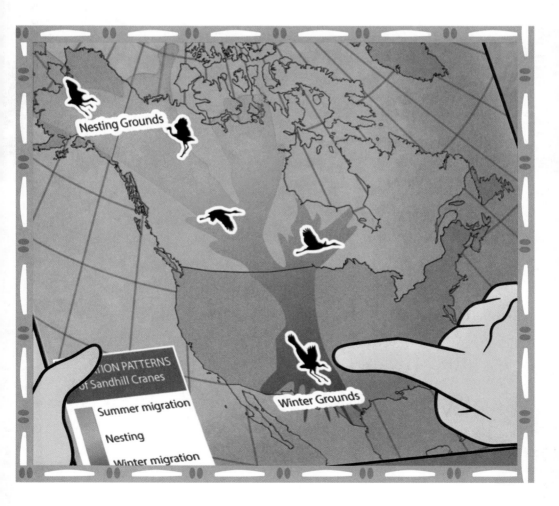

If we don't band any cranes,

we won't know if they made it

to where they're going!

Just then, I think of who can help.

I video-call Grandpa Nat.

"Banding cranes is not easy!"

I tell him.

"Do you have any ideas?"

"Try talking in their language,"
Grandpa Nat suggests.
"When I was a kid, I called to birds
by singing their songs
and dancing their dances!"

I laugh, trying to picture

Grandpa Nat doing a bird dance.

"I gotta see that!" I say.

Grandpa Nat stands up.

He makes a noise.

It sounds like a sandhill crane!

GA-RU-AA! GA-RU-AA!

Grandpa Nat spreads his arms

like they're wings.

Then he hops around.

It looks like fun!

The next day, we try again.

"Astronaut suits . . . check!" I say.

"Beavers fed . . . check!

Dr. Antigone is feeling better . . .

check!"

Next I show everyone

how to sing and dance like a crane.

The cranes seem to like it.

A baby crane comes right up to us!

I hand Dr. Antigone a soft bag.
Dr. Antigone gently places it
on the baby crane's head.
That's so it doesn't get scared.

Dr. Antigone places a band
around the baby crane's leg
and gently tightens it
so the band can't fall off.

The baby crane is banded!

Dr. Antigone removes the bag,

and the baby crane waddles away.

"See you again, *jyah*—little crane!"

I call.

That's one crane banded,

and a bunch more to go.

Time for another crane dance!

Molly's Tips on How to Be a Thoughtful Bird-Watcher

I'm a BIG fan of birds. And lucky for me, Alaska is home to all sorts of birds—cranes, chickadees, puffins, and eagles, to name a few.

Here's how to become a bird-watcher:

1. **Use the right tools.** Binoculars can help you see birds up close, even when you can't get near them. You can also use a field guide to help you identify the birds you see.

2. **Practice listening.** Every bird has its own unique call. It's easier to identify birds when you can see AND hear them.

3. **Bring company!** Bird-watching is a really fun activity, but it's even better with friends.